The Little Circus Kitten

Written by Emma George
Illustrated by Melissa Sweet

GALLERY BOOKS
An Imprint of W. H. Smith Publishers Inc.
112 Madison Avenue
New York City 10016

The day Clancy brought home Minnie Miranda, his friends all gathered around her. "Oh! Ah!" they whispered, trying not to scare her. "Isn't she just the cutest little thing!"

Minnie Miranda wasn't scared. She LOVED
Clancy's friends. She played hide-and-seek with
them until Clancy called, "It's almost show time,
Minnie Miranda. Watch me turn into a clown."

Minnie Miranda LOVED Clancy's trailer.

She made beautiful footprints with his face paint.

She batted his clown nose across the floor.

She licked off a corner of Clancy's smile.

"For such a mini kitten, you're a mighty lot of trouble," sighed Clancy. He tucked her under his bowler hat to keep her out of mischief.

Clancy got into his fire engine and zoomed
into the Tip Top Circus, siren screaming and bell
clanging. The crowd laughed at Clancy. Minnie
Miranda hid under Clancy's hat, sitting on his wig.

Minnie Miranda LOVED that wig. She pawed it and clawed it, and pawed it and clawed it, until Clancy yelled "OUCH!" Clancy yanked off his hat. Minnie Miranda sprang into the air!

"CATCH THAT KITTEN!" yelled Clancy.

Minnie Miranda landed beside an upside-down
acrobat. Minnie Miranda LOVED that acrobat.
She tickled his toes. The acrobat laughed so hard
he fell down. Minnie Miranda dashed into the
next ring.

Clancy ran after her. "CATCH THAT KITTEN!" yelled Clancy.

The crowd laughed until their sides hurt. "What an act!" they gasped.

Minnie Miranda ran to Charla, the elephant. She jumped on Charla's trunk. Minnie Miranda LOVED Charla! She rubbed her head lovingly on Charla's nose. Soon Charla needed to sneeze!

"Ah-ah-ah-CHOOO!" Charla sneezed a sneeze so big that Minnie Miranda shot to the top of the Tip Top Circus tent.

"CATCH THAT KITTEN!" yelled Clancy.

"CATCH THAT KITTEN!" yelled the crowd.

All the actors and animals, acrobats and clowns saw Minnie Miranda sail up through the circus tent air. And all the actors and animals, acrobats and clowns ran to save Minnie Miranda.

Down she came,
and down..
and down...
until...

CRASH! All the actors and animals, acrobats and clowns crashed into each other! They fell down in a silly heap, all except the ringmaster, who caught the falling kitten in his hat!

"INTRODUCING MINNIE MIRANDA!"
bellowed the ringmaster, holding up the kitten
for everyone to see. The crowd loved her!

Minnie Miranda LOVED that crowd. Thank
goodness she was too tired to show it. She fell
asleep the moment Clancy took her back and
tucked her into his big shirt pocket.
    Minnie Miranda ESPECIALLY loved Clancy.